I, *Geronimo Stilton*, have a lot of mouse friends, but none as **spooky** as my friend CREEPELLA VON CACKLEFUR! She is an enchanting and MYSTERIOUS mouse with a pet bat named **Bitewing**. Creepella lives in a CEMETERY, sleeps in a marble **sarcophagus**, and drives a **hearse**. By night she is a special effects and set designer for SCARY FILMS, and by day she's studying to become a journalist! Her father, Boris von Cacklefur, runs the funeral home Fabumouse Funerals, and the von Cacklefur family owns the CREEPY Cacklefur Castle, which sits on top of a skull-shaped mountain in MYSTERIOUS VALLEY.

YIKES! I'm a real 'fraidy mouse, but even I think Creepella and her family are AWFULLY fascinating. I can't wait for you to read this fa-mouse-ly funny and SPECTACULARLY SPOOKY tale!

Geronimo Stilton

Creepella von Cacklefur

Bitewing

Billy Squeakspeare

Grandpa Frankenstein

An extremely mad scientist and an expert in Egyptian mummies.

A journalist who lives in Mysterious Valley and solves spooky cases with her inseparable pet bat, Bitewing.

A famous writer and friend of Creepella.

Shivereen

Grandma Crypt

Snip and Snap

Troublemaking twins and expert spies.

Creepella's favorite niece.

Dolores

Kafka

She loves spiders, and her pet is a gigantic tarantula named Dolores.

The von Cacklefur family's pet cockroach.

Booey the Poltergeist

The mischievous ghost who haunts Cacklefur Castle.

Boneham

The butler to the von Cacklefur family, and a snob right down to the tips of his whiskers.

Baby

He was adopted and raised with love by the von Cacklefurs.

Madame LaTomb

The family housekeeper. A ferocious were-canary nests in her hair.

Chef Stewrat

The cook at Cacklefur Castle. He dreams of creating the ultimate stew.

Boris von Cacklefur

Creepella's father, and the funeral director at Fabumouse Funerals.

Chompers

The von Cacklefur family's meat-eating guard plant.

# Geronimo Stilton

## CREEPELLA VON CACKLEFUR

# THE PHANTOM OF THE THEATER

Scholastic Inc.

Copyright © 2012 by Edizioni Piemme S.p.A., Palazzo Mondadori, Via Mondadori 1, 20090 Segrate, Italy. International Rights © Atlantyca S.p.A. English translation © 2015 by Atlantyca S.p.A.

The publisher does not have any control over and does not assume any responsibility for author or third-party websites or their content.

GERONIMO STILTON names, characters, and related indicia are copyright, trademark, and exclusive license of Atlantyca S.p.A. All rights reserved. The moral right of the author has been asserted. Based on an original idea by Elisabetta Dami. www.geronimostilton.com

Published by Scholastic Inc., 557 Broadway, New York, NY 10012. SCHOLASTIC and associated logos are trademarks and/or registered trademarks of Scholastic Inc.

*Stilton is the name of a famous English cheese. It is a registered trademark of the Stilton Cheese Makers' Association. For more information, go to www. stiltoncheese.com.*

No part of this publication may be reproduced, stored in a retrieval system, or transmitted in any form or by any means, electronic, mechanical, photocopying, recording, or otherwise, without written permission of the copyright holder. For information regarding permission, please contact: Atlantyca S.p.A., Via Leopardi 8, 20123 Milan, Italy; e-mail foreignrights@atlantyca.it, www.atlantyca.com.

This book is a work of fiction. Names, characters, places, and incidents are either the product of the author's imagination or are used fictitiously, and any resemblance to actual persons, living or dead, business establishments, events, or locales is entirely coincidental.

ISBN 978-0-545-75029-5

Text by Geronimo Stilton
Original title *Il fantasma del Teatro dei Sospiri*
Cover by Giuseppe Ferrario (pencils and inks) and Giulia Zaffaroni (color)
Illustrations by Ivan Bigarealla (pencils), Antonio Campro (inks) and Daria Cerchi (color)
Graphics by Yuko Egusa

Special thanks to Joanne Ruelos Diaz
Translated by Anna Pizzelli
Interior design by Becky James

12 11 10 9 8 7 6 5 4 3 2          16 17 18 19 20/0

Printed in the U.S.A.                                    40

First printing, 2016

# No Time for Drama

It was a **splendid** September evening, and all the *New Mouse City* residents were ready to **relax** and let down their fur after a hard day at work. Everybody . . . except yours truly!

But wait! Pardon me. Allow me to introduce myself: My name is Stilton, *Geronimo Stilton*, and I run *The Rodent's Gazette*, the most **FAMOUSE** newspaper on Mouse Island.

It had been a hectic day, and I was as buried under my work as my lasagna gets buried under shredded cheese.

**MOUNTAINS** of paper covered every corner of my desk. I was deciding what to do next — should I *rewrite* an article, or edit a feature, or sift through **PHOTOGRAPHS**? — when my sister, Thea, walked into my office wearing an *elegant* evening gown.

"Still working, Geronimo?" she asked, looking quite bright-eyed and bushy-furred. "I wanted to invite you to the theater!"

Unfortunately, I can't . . .

But it will be fabumouse!

"Unfortunately, I'm up to my SNOUT in work." I sighed. "What show are you going to see?"

Before Thea could answer, my grandfather William Shortpaws **barged** into the room, screaming as usual.

"It's the opera, Grandson! Stop pretending to work and come with us!" he bellowed.

I hadn't yet squeaked a word in reply when my grandfather scurried over to the window. "It's stuffier than a vampire's coffin in here!" he grunted, opening the window.

"**NOOO!**"

I tried to stop him, but it was too late. A ***GUST OF WIND*** from the open window flew past me, and before I knew it, my organized piles of work **swirled** into the air and **tumbled** into one big mess on the floor.

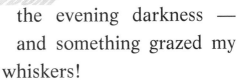

"You are too **MESSY**, Grandson!" said my grandfather, shaking his snout. I got up to close the window, but a flying **SHADOW** appeared through the evening darkness — and something grazed my whiskers!

"Careful where you put your paws, **Cheddarhead**!"

It was **Bitewing**, the pet bat of my friend

CREEPELLA VON CACKLEFUR! She is the most infamouse writer in Mysterious Valley. In his claws, Bitewing was holding a tape recorder, which he flung at me.

"Here you go! It's Creepella's newest **novel**," he screeched. "Publish it IMMEDIATELY,

Aaaa-aaa-AAAAH!

What a voice!

you weak-whiskered rodent!" And with that, he was off.

*FASTER* than a hungry cat chasing a mouse, I turned on the tape recorder.

"**Aaaa-aaa-AAAAH!**" Out came a high-pitched shriek that pierced my eardrums and rattled my eyeglasses.

"I've never heard such a high squeak," Thea said, lowering the paws from her ears.

"But **WHO** can sing like that?" my grandfather wondered.

The tape recorder emitted another sound, even higher pitched than the first one. Thea's paws went right back to her ears.

But I smiled wider than my whiskers. "Thea, Grandfather, sit back on your tails. You are about to listen to one of my most **AMAZING** adventures in Mysterious Valley!"

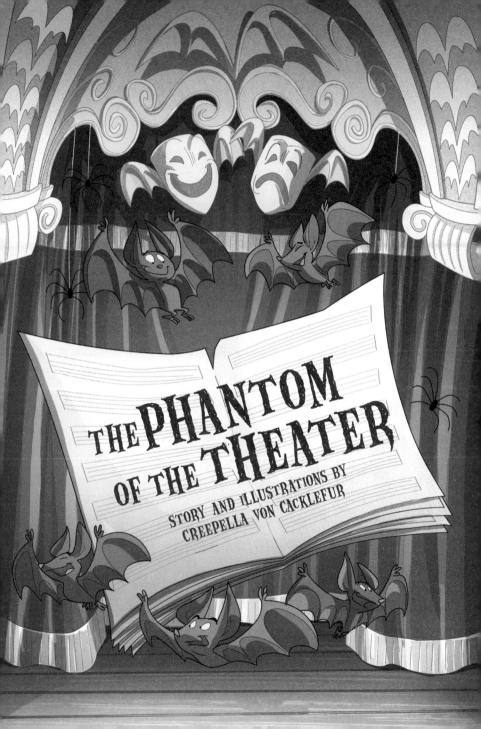

# THE PHANTOM OF THE THEATER

STORY AND ILLUSTRATIONS BY
CREEPELLA VON CACKLEFUR

# A Voice from the Past

CREEPELLA VON CACKLEFUR blotted her lips and gave one last glance to Mirror.

*Ghastly!*

"Ms. Creepella," the talking mirror declared. "Your **Slug Stain Number 5** lipstick really brings out the ghastly glow in your eyes."

*Thank you!*

"Why, thank you, MIRROR," the mouse replied. She took a moment to admire her cheekbones, which were dusted with *Gravestone*

Gray blush, and her eyelashes, elongated with **TERROR AT MIDNIGHT BLUE** mascara.

"While I'm happy to be seen au naturel, I enjoy my deliciously **DREADFUL** makeup too much to be without it!" she said. Now Creepella was **ready** for breakfast, and she bent to pick up the menu that the butler had left for her.

## VON CACKLEFUR BREAKFAST MENU

### FOOD
### (CHALKY AND CRUNCHY!)

* Spoiled milk and tomato oatmeal stew
* Pancakes with bruised bananas and larvae jam
* Horned lizard egg frittata with side of home flies

### DRINKS
### (SCRUMPTIOUSLY SLIMY!)

* Smelly socks smoothie
* Komodo dragon drool shake
* Unlimited stagnant water

"Since Chef Stewrat started training for **top chef: challenge at the DUMP**, he has been preparing spectacularly *disgusting* dishes!" Creepella said, hungrily licking her whiskers. She started to head down to the dining room, but on her way, she realized something was **VERY WRONG**. The pawrail on the stairs was not as dull as it usually was. The **dust** that Madame LaTomb, the housekeeper, took great care in layering on all the furniture each morning was missing. And if that wasn't enough, the **TABLE** in the dining room wasn't set and the youngest von Cacklefur, Baby, was crying furiously.

**WAAAAAAAAAH!**

Chef Stewrat tried to comfort him by feeding him a spoonful of CURDLED cream of wheat stew. "Here you go, sweet ABOMINABLE one. Open up for some Stinky mushy-mush."

"But . . . where is Madame LaTomb?" Creepella asked. It was unusual for Baby to cry without the housekeeper instantly hurrying over.

"She came downstairs with Baby. But once she looked through the mail, her face turned PALER than a block of feta, and she scurried off to her room, leaving me alone with the little one," Chef Stewrat explained.

Creepella was **intrigued**. She went back upstairs to look for Madame LaTomb. When she got to the housekeeper's room, she stuck her snout inside and saw Madame sitting at her vanity, not moving a **whisker**. Creepella cleared her throat and took a few

Oh, dear me!

steps into the room. As she got closer, she noticed that Madame LaTomb was clenching a **C A R D** with a black border.

"Oh, hello, *my dear*. I didn't hear you," Madame said vacantly, not taking her eyes off the card in her paws.

Is something wrong?

"What's going on, Madame? Is something WRONG?" Creepella asked.

Madame LaTomb shook her head, which sent Howler, the were-canary who nested in her hair, flying with a grumble.

"Oh, dear," Madame said, startled. "It's such frightfully fabumouse news that I've been in a daze! Here, read this," she said excitedly, handing Creepella the card.

Creepella began reading the card aloud.

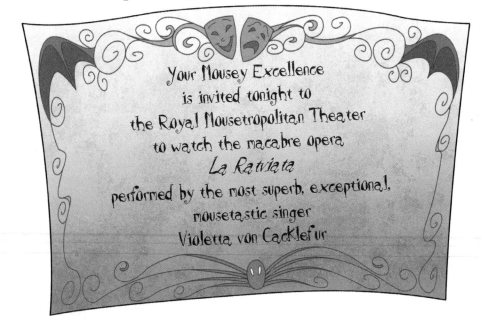

Your Mousey Excellence
is invited tonight to
the Royal Mousetropolitan Theater
to watch the macabre opera
*La Ratviata*
performed by the most superb, exceptional,
mousetastic singer
Violetta von Cacklefur

# ANOTHER VON CACKLEFUR?!

Creepella leaped into the air and twirled around the room. Her whiskers trembled with anticipation. "Violetta von Cacklefur! Rotten ricotta! She is one of our most famouse relatives — and the best opera singer in the world! No mouse can sing high notes like Violetta!"

"I'm so excited, I'm bursting out of my fur!" Madame LaTomb squeaked. "I've loved

La la la LAAAAA!

Violetta von Cacklefur

opera ever since I was a young mouselet. I even used to sing myself — did you know that? When I read the invitation, my heart **MELTED** faster than Brie on burnt toast. I still can't believe it!"

"What's so special about her?" Howler muttered, **grumpy** as usual.

Creepella ignored him completely. "This will be a **WICKEDLY** wonderful, marvemouse event that the whole family must see!"

*So exciting!* *Marvemouse!*

"**Absolutely**!" Madame agreed. "And perhaps we can even go **BACKSTAGE** to say hello before she goes on."

"That's an excellent

idea! Let's tell everyone," Creepella replied.

In *two shakes of a rat's tail*, Madame was calling all the members of the family, and Creepella dashed away to call Geronimo.

"Hello, my little Gerrykins! Get ready — I'm coming to pick you up!" Creepella cackled into the phone as soon as he picked up.

"R-ready? Ready for what? Who is squeaking?" Geronimo asked. It was early, and he hadn't quite woken up.

"Your beloved CREEPELLA, of course! I'm changing our date plans for tonight —"

"D-date? We don't have date plans!" Geronimo interrupted. "We're just going to a movie. But no horror movies, please, because —"

But Creepella took no notice. "We are going to the **darkest** and most MACABRE opera house, the Royal Mousetropolitan Theater!"

"B-but why?"

"And that's not all," Creepella said, dramatically raising the suspense. "My whole family is coming!"

"Argh!" Geronimo blurted. "The whole family?!"

"And what's wrong with that?" Creepella asked in a tone that could freeze a pot of boiling FONDUE.

"N-nothing . . . nothing at all!"

"All right, then. I'm on my way. Dress to impress — from ears to tail. We will be meeting the one and only Violetta von Cacklefur!"

Geronimo was so **surprised** that the phone almost slipped right out of his paws. "Violetta von Cacklefur? **Another** relative? How many mice are in your family?!"

"Oh, Gerry Berry. What a silly question. Go pick out something debonair. I'll be there soon!"

# DIVA IN DESPAIR

The von Cacklefur family gathered outside the *Royal Mousetropolitan Theater* faster than a hungry ratling can eat a cheese baguette. While the show wouldn't start

*Oh, the memories . . .*

for a few hours, Madame LaTomb had arranged to get everyone inside through the back entrance. She guided them confidently through the theater's **MAZE** of hallways.

"I know this theater like the back of my paw," said Madame LaTomb, slowing down to take it all in. "This feels like going **back in time**! You know, when I was young, I met **ARMANDO DI FORMAGGIO**, the great-great-grandson of the **ARCHITECT** who designed the theater," she said fondly.

Armando di Formaggio

"He was a true gentlemouse," she continued, her eyes glazing over like warm **caramel** on a cheesecake.

"A real **rascal**!" Howler screeched. "As **SKINNY** as a skeleton on a diet!"

"Madame, we can scurry down **memory lane** later," Creepella said gently. "But if we want to spend some time with Violetta . . ."

"Yes, yes," Madame said, picking up the pace. They turned a corner. "Ah, here we are!"

The dressing room door was open, and the von Cacklefurs could see Violetta lying on a chair. The family entered quietly on their TIPPY-PAWS so they didn't startle her.

"My dear friend," Madame cried, rushing over to hold the singer's paw. "Whatever is the matter?"

Violetta looked up and studied each member of the family she hadn't seen in ages. Then suddenly, she burst into tears.

"My friends — dear relatives . . . my life is over! I AM RUINED!"

# THE GOLDEN BOX

The most famouse singer in the world looked sadder than a mouse with an empty cheese plate. Her eyes were **RED**, her voice was weak, and her paws were shaky.

"What's going on?" Creepella asked, approaching the distraught singer. Violetta **moaned** and handed Madame LaTomb a golden box. Creepella glanced at its label: **Rich Dark Chocolate Toad Phlegm Truffles**.

"No, thank you, my dear," Madame answered, thinking Violetta was offering her a sweet. "I had a huge *bowl of stew*

Rich Dark Chocolate
Toad Phlegm Truffles

for breakfast."

Violetta shook her snout. "It's all because of these little chocolates. I found them here in my dressing room, and I thought they were a **gift** from a fan. Everyone knows they are my **favorites** . . . I had one, and . . . oh, what a **disaster**!" Violetta cried, dropping her snout into her paws and beginning to weep again.

"What happened after you ate the chocolate?" Creepella prodded.

Violetta's **tears** streamed down her whiskers. "Something terrible! My **high notes** — they've . . .

## DISAPPEARED!"

Violeta gulped and took a deep breath. She opened her mouth wide:

"CROOOOOOOAAAAK!"

Everyone gasped.

"YIKES!"

"YOUR VOICE!"

"This is terrible!"

"What a tragedy!"

"Violetta von Cacklefur needs her high notes!" Madame LaTomb squealed. "An opera singer without her high notes is like an attic with no dust —"

"Or a **SARCOPHAGUS** with no mummy!" Grandpa Frankenstein added.

"Or a **COFFIN** with no corpse," Creepella's

father, Boris von Cacklefur, said, joining in.

"Or my **ꟿꓕꟼꟽ** with no stinky socks," Chef Stewrat mused.

"That's enough!" Creepella exclaimed, giving a scolding look to her family.

"We have to figure out **WHO** sent that

Like a sarcophagus with no mummy . . .

Or a coffin with no corpse . . .

Or my stew with no stinky socks!

box of chocolates to Violetta," Creepella declared. "I smell a **MYSTERY**!"

Geronimo had been keeping quiet, but Creepella's words compelled him to squeak up. "Not only do we have to figure out **WHO** they're from, dear Creepella, but also **WHY** they were sent! Why would someone play this terrible trick on Violetta?"

The singer looked at Geronimo with teary eyes. "I don't know . . ." she whimpered.

In a corner of the dressing room, the black-and-gold wrapping paper that the chocolates came in was crumpled on the floor. Creepella's niece, Shivereen, picked it up and looked at it carefully. A moment later, she let out a squeal.

"Auntie, look at this! A **CARD** is stuck to the wrapping paper!"

Violetta looked over in **confusion**. "I didn't notice anything. I was so eager to unwrap it that I just tossed the paper away."

Creepella opened the card.

"There are two words . . ." she said, studying it. "Ah, it's a **name**!"

"What name?" Geronimo asked.

Creepella squinted as she tried to decipher the handwriting.

BARITONIO
BLACKPONG

Violetta let out a **BLOODCURDLING** scream that sounded like a hundred tortured toads. Then, in a move worthy of the dramatic diva that she was, she put a paw to her forehead and fainted.

CRRRROOOOOOOOOOOOOOAAAK!

Everyone was so captivated by her reaction that they clapped excitedly.

"How elegant!" Grandma Crypt squeaked.

"Such emotion!" Madame LaTomb said breathlessly.

# A BROKEN PROMISE

Grandma Crypt took a SMALL BOTTLE out of her spider-shaped purse. "It's **Slimy Swamp Salts**," she explained. "The stink is strong enough to bring mummies

Slimy Swamp Salts

back to life!" She put the little bottle under Violetta's snout, and she revived instantly.

"Alas, this is all my fault!" Violetta cried out as soon as she came to.

Creepella was beginning to get sick of the mouse's

MELODRAMA. "Can you just tell us why already?" she said, rolling her eyes.

Violetta's tail drooped with despair. "If I had read that name, I would never have eaten those chocolates. My sweet tooth will be my downfall!" she moaned, her paws covering her face.

The family couldn't take it any longer. "**Who is Baritonio Blacksong?!**" they all shouted.

Violetta began **wringing her paws** nervously. Finally, she gulped and took a deep breath. "It's time I told the truth, no matter how DREADFUL it makes me look. I met Baritonio Blacksong many, many years ago. He is the legendary, mysterious, and ghoulish PHANTOM of the Royal Mousetropolitan Theater."

Madame LaTomb's fur stood on end. "The

phantom really exists?!"

Violetta explained. "At the time, I was a promising young singer. I was good, but so were many others. One day, Baritonio appeared in my dressing room and offered to teach me the **SECRET** to singing the *highest* notes. He was stern but very kind. Thanks to his secret lessons, I learned to reach notes higher than any other mouse, even higher than the great Lucia Pawsarotti! Because of him, I got the *lead* role in *Madame Ratterfly*."

The singer paused and sighed. "But on OPENING NIGHT, I did something terrible. Something unforgivable."

Violetta fell **silent**, and Madame LaTomb went to comfort her. "Come sit down, my dear. Take a deep breath."

Violetta followed her friend's advice and

then continued her story. "I had promised Baritonio that during the curtain call at the end of the show, I would **reveal** that he was my teacher, and we would perform the duet from the opera, The Furdresser of Seville. But . . ." the mouse trailed off.

"**But what?!?**" the family shouted in suspense.

"I forgot about it!" Violetta burst out. "I was so overwhelmed by the standing ovation from the audience. I took my bows and walked right **OFF** the stage!

"As soon as I was backstage, I saw Baritonio — as **ANGRY** as a rat **STUNG** by a thousand furious wasps. He had transformed from the kind phantom who had taught me everything I knew into a terrifying **GHOUL**! He whipped out the **secret contract** I had signed. Then he

shook his paw at me and swore he would have **REVENGE**!

"That is why I never came back to GLOOMERIA . . ." Violetta looked up with tears in her eyes. "I had hoped he would have **forgotten** about it by now — but I was wrong."

# LaTomb to the Rescue

Violetta's SOBS shook the whole room. The von Cacklefurs didn't know what to do.

Creepella studied Violetta, then nodded with **DETERMINATION**. "We have no choice," she said. "We have to find the phantom before the show starts!"

Geronimo began to tremble immediately. "W-we? Who's 'we'?"

"Why, cheddar cheeks," Creepella replied, "you and me, of course."

Faster than mold growing on old blue cheese, Geronimo tried to FLEE the dressing room.

But Snip and Snap, the troublemaking twins, TRIPPED him.

"Aaaah!" Geronimo let out a high squeak as he went flying.

"Nice tone!" Grandma Crypt noted.

Geronimo landed with a hard THUD. He knew there was no getting out of helping Creepella. "And wh-what will we do after we find the ph-phantom?" he stammered as he got back to his paws.

"Elementary, my dear Stilton," Creepella cooed. "We convince him to forgive Violetta and give her back her voice!"

The other von Cacklefurs chimed in with approval. "Excellent idea!"

However, Geronimo wasn't convinced. He stood up, dusted off his jacket, and asked, "Creepella, in the name of all things cheesy, do you have the slightest idea

where Baritonio is hiding?"

Creepella looked at her furry friend with supreme confidence. "Of course not. That's why we have to find him!"

Violetta interrupted them with a weak voice. "The theater is . . . *sniff* . . . huge. The BASEMENT alone is filled with closets and passagewdys . . . *sniff* . . . that no one but Baritonio knows about . . ."

"ALMOST no one!" squealed Madame LaTomb.

"Almost no one!" screeched Howler.

*Almost no one!* The von Cacklefurs, Geronimo, and Violetta stared at the housekeeper with puzzled expressions.

"As I told you, I met ARMANDO DI FORMAGGIO, the great-great-grandson of the ARCHITECT of the theater," Madame explained.

"Useless bag of bones . . ." Howler muttered.

"One day, he took me to what used to be his great-great-grandfather's office," the housekeeper went on. "In an **old** trunk, he had found a **MAP** of the theater, which we both studied. Violetta is right that the

basement is a real **MAZE**. But I still remember where the entrance is, and I can lead you to it!"

Creepella wasted no time. She pushed Geronimo out the door, shouting, "Shivereen! Bitewing! You're coming with us. The show is starting shortly. Let's scurry!"

However, Bitewing was already making himself comfortable hanging upside down from the chandelier. "I wanted to take a nap!" he protested.

Creepella threw the bat a **gummy beetle**, which he snapped right up.

"Mmm . . ." Bitewing flew to the door as he gulped down the treat. "You've convinced me. **LET'S GOOOO!**"

Gummy beetle treat

# TRICK OR TREAT?

The dressing rooms lined a **long hallway** that ended with a tiny door. It was painted the same color as the wall and had no knob. They wouldn't have noticed it at all if Madame LaTomb hadn't stopped and pointed to it. "Here's the ENTRANCE to the basement. I'm sure of it!"

On the door was written:

STEP RIGHT IN, AND USE YOUR SNOUT.
BUT ONCE YOU'RE IN, YOU CAN'T COME OUT!

"It's a line from one of my favorite operas, **RATOLETTO** by Giuseppe Mousi!" Madame LaTomb exclaimed. Creepella pushed the door **fiercely**, but it didn't budge.

"Hmm," Creepella thought aloud. "There's no knob or lock. There has to be another **MECHANISM** to open the door . . . but what is it?"

*"Step right in, and use your* **SNOUT**. *But once you're in,* **YOU CAN'T COME OUT** . . ." Madame LaTomb sang quietly. *"An* eternity *of fears awaits. Find the* key. *Unlock your fate!"*

Suddenly, the door **CLICKED** and **POPPED** open.

"The unlocking mechanism must be voice activated!" Creepella exclaimed. "By singing the lyrics, you cracked the **CODE**!"

Creepella pushed open the door farther to discover a steep spiral staircase.

She took a few steps and called back to the others. "Careful — the steps are a little rotten." Shivereen and Madame LaTomb followed Creepella on light paws. As Geronimo trailed them, one of the steps gave out. His paw went straight through it.

"Ack! A little rotten?! The steps are completely rotten!" he screeched, clambering to get free.

Help!

Hee, hee!

"Oh, hush, you scaredy-mouse,"
Creepella said with a snort from the
bottom of the stairs. She pulled out
the *flashlight* Grandpa Frankenstein had
given her on her birthday. She
turned it on and waved
a **SPIDER-SHAPED**
beam of light around
the area.

They were in a
small room, and in
front of them was
a big **STEEL
DOOR** covered
with thick chains
and a huge lock. The
walls were draped with
thick **SPIDERWEBS** woven
in beautifully intricate patterns. Madame

LaTomb was mesmerized. "Who could have woven these?" she marveled.

Creepella directed the flashlight to a corner of the room and revealed the answer.

There was a **HUGE HAIRY SPIDER** sitting on top of a key ring! Its **RED** eyes scrutinized the newcomers.

"What an adorable little critter!" Shivereen gushed. She approached the spider, holding her paw out toward it.

"Careful! Better not to trust a strange spider," Creepella said. "I have Kafka's

B-but it's huge!

Fetch!

cockroach crunchies in my pocket. Let's see if it likes them."

She tossed one to the spider, who snatched it out of the air and gobbled it right up.

Creepella then threw one crunchie after another across the room, each one a bit farther than the last. The enoRMouse spider followed the treats, moving away from the corner little by little and leaving the keys EXPOSED. As it munched another crunchie, Creepella shouted, "Shivereen, now! Grab the keys!"

Her niece snatched up the keys, RAN to the door, and unlocked the bolt. All the mice rushed through it, leaving the well-fed SPIDER behind them.

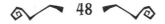

# TRA-LA-LA! RIDDLE-DEE-DEE!

Creepella aimed her flashlight in front of the group and ILLUMINATED a long, narrow, seemingly endless **tunnel**.

"D-do we h-have to go in there?" asked Geronimo.

"Most definitely," Creepella insisted. "We can *only* go forward," she said, **strutting** down the tunnel.

"B-but why?" Geronimo stammered.

Creepella snorted. "**Cheesy pie**, must I explain everything? Everyone knows that once you enter a **DARK** tunnel like this, you can only go forward. Otherwise, you

end up getting **trapped**! I learned this my very first year of the Acad —"

# THUMP!

"What was **THAT**?" Shivereen asked.

"The fur-face has fainted!" Bitewing snickered.

Creepella knew just what to do. "No need to **panic**. Luckily, Grandma Crypt gave me her bottle of **Slimy Swamp Salts**." She swiftly pulled it out and waved it under Geronimo's nose.

He came to so fast it was as if he'd been dumped into the frigid waters of the Ratlantic Ocean. Instead of fear, a look of utter disgust had taken over his face.

"What is that HORRIFIC smell?!" he cried, furiously rubbing his snout with the back of his paw.

"Why, a delightfully dreadful perfume!" Creepella replied while Shivereen, Madame LaTomb, and Howler nodded behind her in agreement.

Geronimo walked quickly to get away from the stink.

What is that smell?!

Finally, the long hallway ended in a large, round room with a small blocked door. Creepella directed her light to the door and noticed a **yellowed note** stuck to it with a **skull-shaped pin.**

The fearless mouse took it down and read:

MUSICAL RIDDLES
Tra-la-la! Riddle-dee-dee!
Solve them all or never be free!

"**RIDDLES?!** What if we can't figure them out?!" Geronimo said, whiskers trembling. "We'll be stuck here **forever**!"

"Don't worry your **pretty little fur**," his friend answered. "We can't have you faint aga —"

But it was too late. Geronimo had already collapsed.

Creepella groaned.
"We're out of smelling salts!"

"Don't worry, my dear," Madame LaTomb said reassuringly. "**Bitewing** will take care of him." The housekeeper shot a stern glance at the bat. "In the meantime, we have to figure out these **RIDDLES**!"

When Geronimo came to, he was **SHOCKED** to find out that the riddles had all been solved.

"B-but how?" the mouse stuttered.

"Gerry Berry, riddles are **NO MATCH FOR ME**," Creepella said casually. "All we had to do was figure out all the

# MUSICAL RIDDLES

1. I have eighty-eight keys, but there's no door I can open. What am I?

2. I'm an instrument that a skeleton might play. What am I?

3. I'm a type of band that doesn't play music. What am I?

4. You can play me best when you hold me by the neck. What am I?

5. I have strings you can't tie and a bow that is straight. What am I?

6. No one's scales are better than mine. What am I?

7. I'm an instrument you can hear but can't touch or see. What am I?

8. I'm a part of your head where you can play the best rhythms. What am I?

9. I am a phone that plays the best songs. What am I?

answers, say them in a loud voice to **activate** the unlocking mechanism — because, as we know, everything down here works through vocal commands — and the door opened. **Piece of cheesecake!**" She took a moment to give a smile of satisfaction.

"Now, let's **shake a tail**! I'm sure we're close to **GETTING OUT** of this maze!"

# ROYAL MOUSETROPOLITAN THEATER BASEMENT
Find the way through the maze to get to Baritonio Blacksong!

# EMBRACE YOUR DOOM!

To Creepella's surprise, finding their way through the maze proved **HARDER** than finding a moldy cheese slice in a haystack. After many, many attempts scurrying up and down the labyrinth of passageways, the mice **finally** found their way to the other side of the theater basement. Unfortunately, Baritonio was still **nowhere** to be found.

"We'll never get out of here!" Geronimo wailed.

Instead, the mice found yet **another** locked door with **another** note attached to it with a skull-shaped pin. Creepella read

the shaky handwriting:

> One step from your tomb,
> Don't try to be brave.
> Embrace your doom.

Geronimo stared at the note. "**GREAT CHUNKS OF CHEDDAR!** What in the name of string cheese does this mean?"

Creepella twirled her tail thoughtfully. "I'm not sure yet, my handsome Havarti . . ."

"Maybe it's another verse to a song!" Shivereen suggested. "If we sing the next verse, we could trigger the unlocking mechanism, just like with the other doors."

Madame LaTomb began to nod her head sadly. "You're right . . . it's a song from Ratcido Domingo's least successful opera, MOUSE OF LA NACHO. It's about

a mouse who eats nachos that he knows are **poisonous**, but he can't stop himself. Whoever wrote this note is an **expert**. I can't remember how the rest of the song goes!"

"Try, Madame, try!" pleaded Geronimo. "Or else we'll never get out of here!"

The housekeeper closed her eyes and tried to will the words into her **BRAIN**. But they wouldn't come.

"N-now what do we d-do?" Geronimo stammered, starting to **sway**.

"**DON'T FAINT!**" Creepella shouted.

"Maybe we could think of a word that **rhymes** with 'brave' to help Madame remember the words to the next line," suggested Shivereen.

"That's a **mousefastic** idea!" Creepella replied. "Let's think. **Wave** rhymes with **brave** . . ."

"**Cave**, **pave**, **rave** . . ." Geronimo offered.

"**Shave**, **crave** . . ." Shivereen tried.

The mice were interrupted when Howler **JETTED** out of Madame LaTomb's hair. "You three are **terribly** amusing," the were-canary said with a chilly shrill. "Too bad you could fit **MOUNT RATVEREST**

Howler, what is it?

Tell us! Tell us!

between you and the solution." Everyone stared at him, annoyed but hopeful.

"Does that mean YOU know what comes next?" Geronimo asked urgently.

"But of course! I know every verse in every song of every opera. There is no better singer than me. Not even Violetta von Cacklefur —"

Now it was Madame LaTomb's turn to jump in. "For Gouda's sake, Howler, don't be RUDE! And STOP wasting time!" she said reproachfully. "If you know the song, sing it at once!"

Howler GLARED at Madame for a moment, grumbling quietly. Then he took a deep breath, puffed out his chest, and howled:

"One step from your tomb,
Don't try to be brave.

EMBRACE YOUR DOOM.
YOU CAN'T AVOID YOUR GRAVE!
GHOULS AND GOBLINS
WILL SOON START TO ARRIVE
TO HAUNT YOUR COFFIN!
YOU WON'T COME OUT ALIVE!"

And as slowly as a mouse savors his last piece of cheese, the door creaked open.

# REVENGE, SWEET REVENGE!

A large room with an **enoRMouSe** bed and a wardrobe piled high with **clothes** and accessories awaited Creepella and company. Inside the wardrobe, hundreds of *beautiful* dresses hung on the racks.

"These are all the stage costumes!" Madame exclaimed. "This is from *The Jealous Coffinmaker* starring Chordelia Callas. And this is from Mousezart's **THE MACABRE FLUTE!**"

"How fabumouse!" Creepella exclaimed. "I love the little embroidered **BATS** on that one."

In one corner was a gramophone and piles of **dusty old records**. Madame stooped down to take a closer look. "This really is an enviable collection," she noted.

On a round table next to the records, Shivereen found a **BIG RED BOOK**. She leafed through it and saw pages and pages of pictures and articles about Violetta. Someone had compiled all the clippings about the singer from the last few years.

"Look what I found, Auntie. One of Violetta's biggest admirers must live here," she said, holding up the book.

"Hm . . . You may be right! Or perhaps this rodent has become an ex-admirer," Creepella pondered.

"Congratulations!" **BOOMED** an unfamiliar voice. BARITONIO BLACKSONG

# BARITONIO BLACKSONG'S ROOM

WATCH OUT! CREEPELLA AND FRIENDS ARE NOT ALONE!
CAN YOU FIND BLACKSONG?

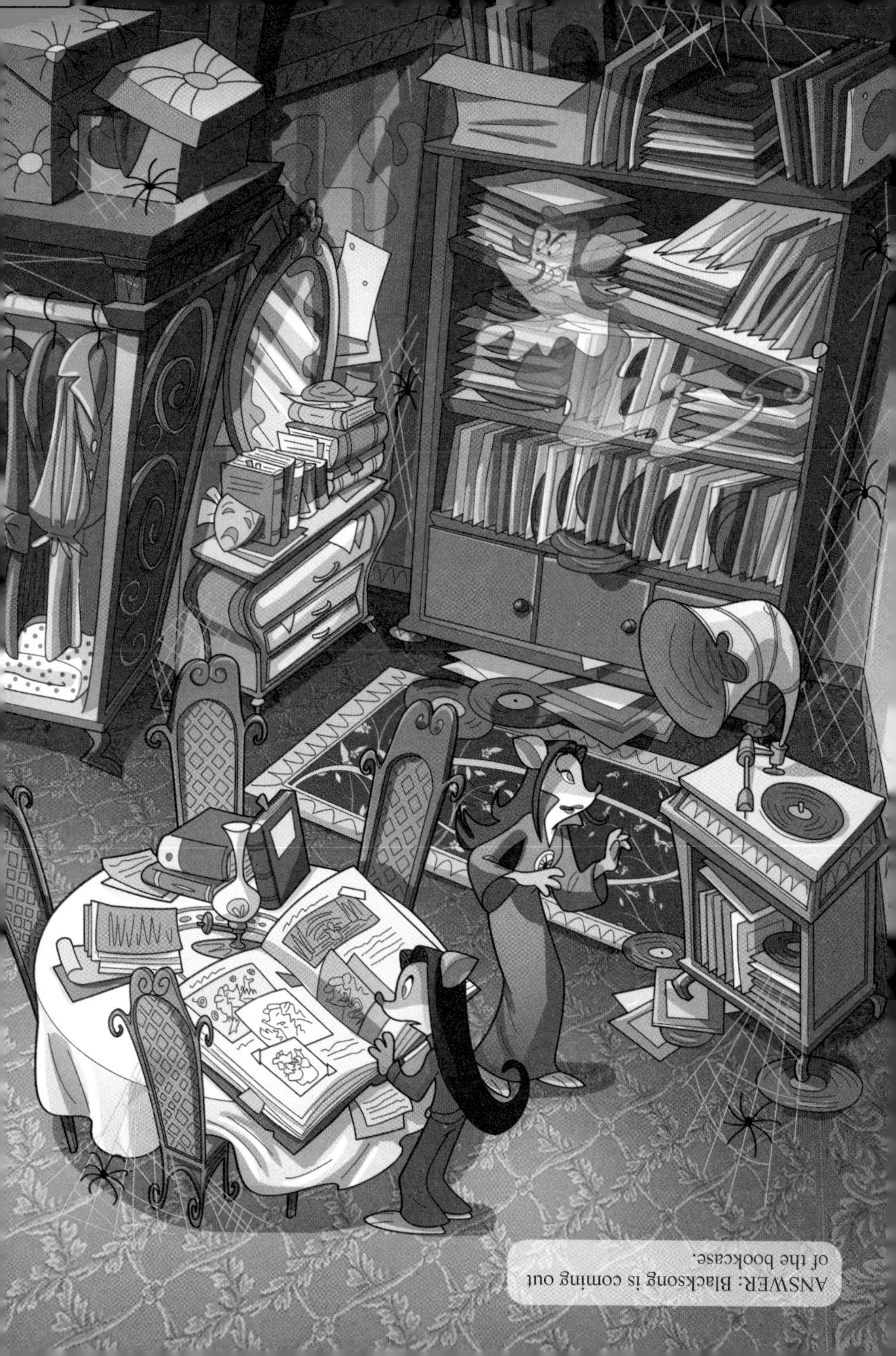

ANSWER: Blacksong is coming out of the bookcase.

_Congratulations!_

appeared in front of the bookcase and took a bow. "No mouse has ever managed to get this far. You solved all my TRICKY PUZZLES. You deserve a special prize . . ."

His words were kind, but the mice felt **shivers** down their tails.

Creepella proceeded with caution. "We don't want a prize. What we want is for you to give back Violetta's high notes."

Blacksong's nose wrinkled, and then he took a **letter** out of his pocket and handed it to Creepella with a strange look. "This is the **promise** that Violetta made to me many years ago. You can still smell her

rotten **violet** perfume on it. Read it and you will understand . . ."

Creepella didn't move a whisker, so Geronimo took the letter instead.

"No, don't!" Creepella said, **EYEING** the letter suspiciously.

However, Geronimo was more curious than a **CAT**, and he immediately read the letter.

"Actually, listen to this," Geronimo said. "The phantom is not completely **wrong** for being angry."

*No, don't!*

Geronimo read aloud the **agreement** written and signed by Violetta: "Without the **PHANTOM**,

Baritonio Blacksong, I would never have been able to sing the *highest notes* of any mouse. I **swear** that tonight I will tell the world about his generosity by singing the duet from . . ."

As the mouse continued, Creepella noticed that Blacksong's grin was growing. "Gerrykins, stop! Stop reading! Don't you see?!" she yelped.

But it was too late. ". . . *The Furdresser of Seville,*" Geronimo finished.

"Noooo!" Creepella cried.

The floor beneath them **OPENED UP**. A trapdoor swung down, sending the mice FALLING. They landed on the floor of a cold, dark cell with a loud and painful **CRASH**!

"Do you have mold for brains?" Howler shouted. "By reading the letter, you

**activated** the voice command for the trapdoor!"

Up above, they heard the phantom cackling. **"REVENGE! SWEET, SWEET REVENGE!** I will never forgive that ungrateful mouse. Tonight she will learn the lesson she deserves!"

Nooooo!

# A Captive Audience

"Everything **HURTS**!" Geronimo moaned. "Even my whiskers hurt." But with one glance from Creepella, he shut his snout. This was the least of their problems.

They were in an **UNDERGROUND PRISON**, where no mouse would ever want to set paw.

"This is what happens when you stick your snout into someone else's business!" Baritonio called down to them. "Now there's nothing stopping my REVENGE PLAN. In a few minutes, Violetta will step on stage and give the **worst** performance of her life! And YOU will be my HONORED

My revenge!

GUESTS for it."
Creepella sneered.
"And how will we be
able to see anything
from down here?"
she said with a
defiant look.

Let us out!

"Look to your right," the phantom replied. "Open that little **WiNDOW** and you will have your answer."

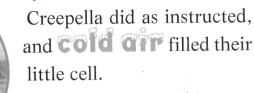

Creepella did as instructed, and **cold air** filled their little cell.

"What is it?" Shivereen asked as she put her paw through the opening.

"It's a **tube** that connects directly to the stage," Baritonio explained. "Don't even think about escaping through it. It's much **too small**. But you will be able to **hear** what happens above perfectly. I used to **feed lines** to that ungrateful Violetta when she **forgot** them. Even that opening night, I reminded her of her promise. But the applause apparently made **MOLD** grow in her ears!"

Madame LaTomb tried to **DEFEND** her friend. "But she has always been sorry. She wants to make up for what she did to you!"

Baritonio grunted. "You must be **JOKING**. The only thing she cares about is forever sounding like a warty

We can hear the audience!

toad. I can't wait to hear her **CROAK**!

The chill in Baritonio's laughter could have frozen even the GLACIERS in the Mountains of the Mangy Yeti, but the chanting of the audience in the theater silenced it.

"Violetta! Violetta! We want Violetta!"

Baritonio's ears twitched. "Now I must leave you. Your **friend** is coming onstage, and I don't want to miss a moment!

The phantom closed the trapdoor, and

**DARKNESS** filled the cell. But despite the despair of their current situation, the friends had only one thought:

Poor Violetta!

# THE SHOW MUST GO ON

Meanwhile, back in Violetta's DRESSING ROOM, the other von Cacklefurs were getting nervous.

"Where can they be?" GRANDMA CRYPT repeated for the hundredth time.

"They should have found him by now!" GRANDPA FRANKENSTEIN exclaimed.

"Baritonio has probably captured them, and it's all my fault!" Violetta bawled, but without her high notes, her sobs sounded like vomiting toads.

"CRRROOOAAAK! CRROOOAAAK, CROOOAAAK!"

Snip and Snap, who had gotten hold of the **chocolates** when no one was looking, had eaten three each, and now they, too, were **croaking**.

"Enough!" cried Boris von Cacklefur. "It's louder than a SWAMP full of toads at an all-the-flies-you-can-eat buffet! BE QUIET, or I'll tie your tails together!"

Then someone **knocked** on the dressing room door. It was the theater director coming to get Violetta.

I'll tie your tails together!

Croooak!

Croak!
Croak!

"The theater is **PACKED**!" he announced, his paws shaking. "Every seat is filled — from the orchestra to the balconies. All of GLOOMERIA is here to see the great Violetta. We **abso-mousely** cannot wait any longer!"

*The show must go on!*

The von Cacklefurs tried to convince the director to stall for a few more minutes, but it was no use. "If we don't start immediately, the audience will riot! It will be a CAT-ASTROPHE!"

Violetta stood up slowly as if she were carrying a heavy GRAVESTONE on her back. "The director is right. I can't keep the audience waiting any longer."

"But what will you do about your high

notes?" asked a worried Grandma Crypt.

Instead of replying, Violetta **slunk** out the dressing room door. Grandma Crypt shot glances at the others, and they all followed her. When the family realized she was heading toward the **STAGE**, they nervously went to take their seats in the audience.

Every mouse in Gloomeria really did seem to be at the show. In the second row, the entire Rattenbaum family sat smugly. Grandpa Frankenstein stiffened when his eyes locked with Shamley Rattenbaum.

"Those **moldy sewer rats** can't wait to see one of the von Cacklefurs make a fool of herself!" Grandpa whispered.

Grandma Crypt shifted in her seat and **sighed**. "I just wish I knew where the others were."

A loud round of applause broke into her thoughts, and the CURTAIN lifted, revealing Violetta CENTER STAGE.

Violetta had the attention of every mouse in the theater, including one hidden from view. Behind a heavy curtain on the farthest corner of the stage, Baritonio was watching the singer, as still as a CORPSE.

# THE LAST
# LOCK

"**GReat cHeeSe BaLLS of fiRe!**
We have to get out of here!" Creepella fumed, examining the walls with her paws for the millionth time to try to find an opening.

"We've searched every **nook and cranny** of this cell, my dear Creepella," Geronimo said, trying to soothe her. "There is nothing left we can do."

Howler and Bitewing agreed. They had tried to fly through the **tunnel** that led to the stage, but a net **blocked** the way, and they had to come back.

Then Creepella, Geronimo, Madame

I can't reach!

Just a little more!

Higher!

Oof!

Grunt!

LaTomb, and Shivereen had tried to **climb** on top of one another to reach the trapdoor in the ceiling, but it was **TOO** high and **TOO** tightly closed. They might as well have had their paws **TIED** behind their backs. Violetta was about to making a laughingstock of herself in front of all the rodents of GLOOMERIA, and they couldn't help at all.

The audience's

thunderous applause alerted them that the singer had reached the stage.

"What will she do?" Shivereen squeaked.

"I can't bear to listen!" Madame LaTomb said, shutting her EYES tight and covering her ears with her paws.

The applause died down and was replaced with an eerie silence. The orchestra started to play, and Violetta's melodious voice filled the air.

"Sing once again with me,
my perfect rat.
Your squeals will keep away
those evil cats.
When the moon shines tonight,
with song, we'll fight!"

Suddenly, Madame LaTomb's eyes *flashed* open. "It's time! The *high note* is coming!" she said, gripping her tail.

The high note, however, never came. Violetta was so anxious that she **fainted** right on the stage.

Creepella and the others strained their ears and heard her being picked up and carried back to her **DRESSING ROOM**. When several minutes had passed and the singer didn't return to the stage, the audience started to boo.

"Boooo!"
"We want our money back!"
"Violetta is a phony!"

"Ohhh, poor, poor Violetta!" Madame LaTomb cried. "She's **doomed**!"

The WERE-CANARY stalked out of his hair nest with a spiteful look. "Well, I can't say she didn't deserve it . . ."

"She made a mistake," Shivereen said thoughtfully. "But Baritonio could have **forgiven** her by now . . . it's been such a long time."

Geronimo shook his snout in agreement. "You're right. I've never met a mouse who's acted so **heartlessly**, even a ghost." He paused. "But he must have a heart deep inside. It's just locked away . . ."

On hearing those words, Creepella yelped. "You're a genius, Gerrycakes! Baritonio's heart is just locked away! To make him open up and feel again, we need to find the right song. We can fix this!"

"FIX THIS! FIX THIS! FIX THIS!" Bitewing squeaked.

Geronimo looked at Creepella in confusion. "But how . . . ?"

Creepella smiled. "Didn't you hear what the phantom said? He said he used to whisper lines to Violetta when she forgot the words onstage."

"So?" prodded Geronimo.

"So, that means the **tunnel** carries sound from here to the stage! All we have to do is sing a song that will remind Baritonio of how he loved singing with Violetta, and he'll forgive her!"

"I wish I could help, but I'm as tone-deaf as a cat's yowl," Geronimo said. "You'd have better luck with a clanging bell!"

Creepella smirked. "I'm not counting on either of us to save the day this time."

# A Song for Baritonio

Back ONSTaGE, the theater director was trying to calm the audience. "Ladies and gentlemice, I am pleased to announce that in tonight's opera, Violetta von Cacklefur will be replaced by the mezzo-soprano Wynona B. Flatfur, fresh off her debut at the Wrong Note Theater — aaaah!" He ducked to avoid a bunch of rancid broccoli hurtling toward the stage, which was quickly followed by MOLDY CAULIFLOWER and mushy ROTTEN TOMATOES.

Seizing the opportunity, Chef Stewrat rushed to the stage to pick up the food.

"Mmm! So many delicious ingredients for my stew!" he said with glee.

The rest of the audience was **FURIOUS**. They were so upset, it took a few minutes for them to hear the MELODY coming from the theater's **basement**. Then slowly, one after another, they were captivated by Madame LaTomb's voice.

The von Cacklefurs' housekeeper had picked an emotional song to reach the heart of the mouse holding her dear friend's voice hostage: "Sorry Rotten Heart" from the opera *Don Rattovani*.

"MY TRULY DREADFUL FRIEND,
SHE HIDES AWAY IN FEAR.
SILENT MUCH TOO LONG,
FOR ALL THESE MOLDY YEARS.
MANY MOONS HAVE PASSED;
SHE'S SUNG TOO MANY SONGS.
BUT NOW IT'S TIME FOR HER
TO RIGHT HER MANY WRONGS."

As Madame let the last notes of the verse trail off, a heavy silence filled the air.

Then suddenly, a roar of applause filled the theater. The audience was on its feet, cheering for the MYSTERIOUS voice.

Down in the prison cell, Baritonio Blacksong appeared out of nowhere and knelt in front of Madame LaTomb.

"My dear Madame! What a haunting voice!" he bellowed, grabbing the housekeeper's paws between his own. "What a sublime interpretation! It has been decades since I've heard singing like this. I had forgotten how moving a song could be!

I bow to such a great artist!

I bow to such a great artist!"

Howler peeked his head out of his mistress's hair. "I taught her everything she knows."

The phantom blew his nose with an invisible handkerchief before blubbering, "I would do anything for you, Madame!"

Madame LaTomb smiled so wide, even her whiskers turned up. This was the moment they'd been waiting for. "All I ask is that my friend Violetta get her high notes back," she said decidedly.

Anticipating Baritonio's resistance, Creepella hurried to add, "She's very sorry for what she did to you!"

The prisoners held their breaths as they watched Baritonio tremble with emotion. No one moved a whisker.

"All right, let's go to her," he replied.

# SAVE THE SOPRANO!

Baritonio led the small group through a shortcut that only he knew.

"This theater is really incredible!" Geronimo gushed, invigorated by his freedom. "They should organize some guided tours!"

"You like it now that you know you're not trapped here forever, you scaredy-rat!" Howler teased.

Madame pushed the were-canary back into her hair with a small but forceful SHOVE.

On the other side of the theater, the rest of the von Cacklefur family surrounded

Violetta as she lay on her sofa hiding under a blanket. "Oh! What a disaster! What a disaaaaaster!" she moaned.

The family was starting to think Violetta would never recover when CREEPELLA and the others came bursting into the room.

What a disaster!

Poor Violetta . . .

It's not funny!

They were even more surprised when the **PHANTOM** Baritonio dashed past them all to kneel by Violetta's side.

"Does this ghost do anything but kneel down?" Shivereen wondered.

"Another **softy**," Bitewing concluded.

"Oh, dear Violetta! Please **forgive** me!" Baritonio pleaded.

"Baritonio?" Violetta whispered. She couldn't believe it. "Oh, please forgive ME!" she begged, touching her **heart** with her paw.

Madame sighed. "What a **disgustingly** moving moment," she said, dabbing away **tears**.

Out in the main theater, the audience was not sharing in any tender moments. They were still demanding a **ShoW**!

Baritonio handed Violetta a small box. "Take two **chocolate-**

**covered toad's warts**, and you'll get your high notes back, my dear."

Violetta **nervously** ate the candy. Then she took a deep breath and sang a high C.

"Aaaa-ahhhh-eeeeee!"

"It worked!" Creepella exclaimed. "Violetta can **sing** again! The show can be saved!"

The singer smiled. "It can, but not by me alone. **Two friends** will have to sing with me."

Aaaa-ahhh-eeeeee!

# HAPPILY GLOOMY EVER AFTER

"Encore! Encore! Encore!"

When Violetta, Baritonio, and Madame LaTomb took the stage, the audience wasn't sure what to expect. But from the trio's first note squealed in perfectly gruesome harmony, they were mesmerized. With each new song, the singers transported the audience further into a terrifically **dark and dreary** paradise.

"It is the most horrifically fabumouse show I've ever seen!" Geronimo whispered.

He, like everyone else, had practically clapped the **FUR** right off his paws. Every time the singers tried to leave the stage, the audience stomped and squealed until they were forced to come back onstage to sing another song. After **ten encores**, the show finally ended because the crowd was hoarse from cheering.

Laaaaaaaa!

Laaaaaaaaaa!

Laaaaaaaaaaaaaa!

After the show, it was almost **impossible** to get into Violetta's dressing room. Bouquets of **rotten flowers** were piled high along every wall.

The singer could not stop thanking her family and friends. "Without you, my career — **MY LIFE!** — would be over!" she gushed.

Thank you, friends!

Bravo!

"And now I have some **exciting news**," she continued. "Gloomeria witnessed the incredible Baritonio Blacksong tonight. It would be a **great loss** if his voice was not heard again. And since singing with him has made me so **happy** —"

"We have decided to go on a **WORLD**

Now, who's hungry?

What a show!

TOUR together!" the phantom finished.

"Hooray!" The room full of mice cheered.

With so much to celebrate, it was a long night. It was very, very late when the von Cacklefurs finally made their way home.

"I'm going to put Baby to bed," Madame LaTomb announced. "GOOD NIGHTMARES, everyone!"

"Madame," Geronimo called out. "Why don't you JOIN the tour with Violetta and Baritonio? You're a stupendous trio!"

The housekeeper looked lovingly around the room. "No," she replied while giving Baby a tight squeeze. "I have everything I need right here at Cacklefur Castle. I couldn't imagine being this happily gloomy anywhere else!"

THE END

# THE WORLD TOUR

On the tape recorder, Creepella's voice **faded away** and was replaced with background static. I had been in a dream state listening to her describe that **THRILLING NIGHT** at the Royal Mousetropolitan Theater. The crackling sounds snapped me back to my office in New Mouse City.

Grandfather William and Thea were pumped up.

"Geronimo, this story had me on the edge of my seat. It's a true paw-biter," my sister declared. "Publish it immediately!"

"Yes, **you must**," my grandfather

concurred. "You're a huge scaredy-mouse in the story, but —"

I was about to squeak that I'd like to see how he would have acted in my place when CREEPELLA'S shrill voice chirped back out of the tape recorder.

"Well, furheart, I'm sure you're already thinking about when you can publish this gripping story, but it'll have to wait a few

What a thrill!

Bravo!

You 'fraidy rat!

days. Tomorrow, Violetta and Baritonio are kicking off their world tour, *The Phantom of the Theater*, at the Royal Mousetropolitan Theater, and they are counting on you to be there. Invite whomever you wish and get here right away!"

A **click** signaled the end of the tape.

"Well!" Grandfather **BELLOWED**. "What are you waiting for?! You heard her. We better get going!"

He was right. Violetta's and Baritonio's voices had **haunted** me ever since that night, and I couldn't wait to hear them again. And once the performance was over, I would publish Creepella's book straightaway. I knew we had another **BESTSELLER** on our paws, because there's no better suspense writer in Mysterious Valley than CREEPELLA VON CACKLEFUR!

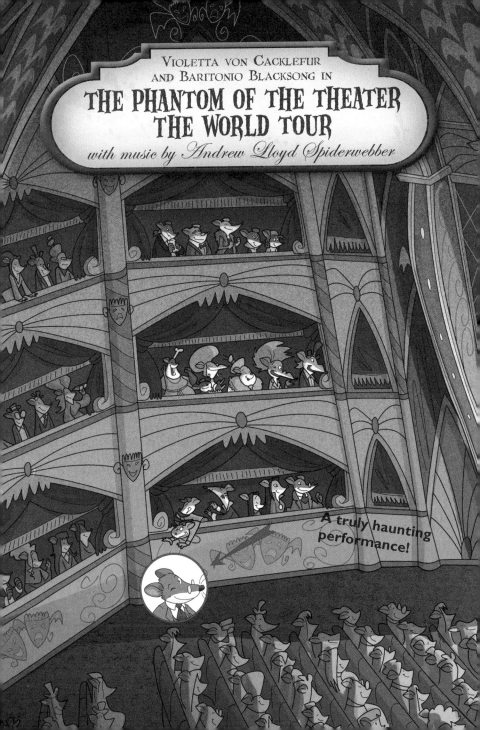

# If you liked this book, be sure to check out my other adventures!

**#1 THE THIRTEEN GHOSTS**

**#2 MEET ME IN HORRORWOOD**

**#3 GHOST PIRATE TREASURE**

**#4 RETURN OF THE VAMPIRE**

**#5 FRIGHT NIGHT**

**#6 RIDE FOR YOUR LIFE!**

**#7 A SUITCASE FULL OF GHOSTS**

**#8 THE PHANTOM OF THE THEATER**

# Be sure to read all my fabumouse adventures!

#1 Lost Treasure of the Emerald Eye

#2 The Curse of the Cheese Pyramid

#3 Cat and Mouse in a Haunted House

#4 I'm Too Fond of My Fur!

#5 Four Mice Deep in the Jungle

#6 Paws Off, Cheddarface!

#7 Red Pizzas for a Blue Count

#8 Attack of the Bandit Cats

#9 A Fabumouse Vacation for Geronimo

#10 All Because of a Cup of Coffee

#11 It's Halloween, You 'Fraidy Mouse!

#12 Merry Christmas, Geronimo!

#13 The Phantom of the Subway

#14 The Temple of the Ruby of Fire

#15 The Mona Mousa Code

#16 A Cheese-Colored Camper

#17 Watch Your Whiskers, Stilton!

#18 Shipwreck on the Pirate Islands

#19 My Name Is Stilton, Geronimo Stilton

#20 Surf's Up, Geronimo!

**#21 The Wild, Wild West**

**#22 The Secret of Cacklefur Castle**

**A Christmas Tale**

**#23 Valentine's Day Disaster**

**#24 Field Trip to Niagara Falls**

**#25 The Search for Sunken Treasure**

**#26 The Mummy with No Name**

**#27 The Christmas Toy Factory**

**#28 Wedding Crasher**

**#29 Down and Out Down Under**

**#30 The Mouse Island Marathon**

**#31 The Mysterious Cheese Thief**

**Christmas Catastrophe**

**#32 Valley of the Giant Skeletons**

**#33 Geronimo and the Gold Medal Mystery**

**#34 Geronimo Stilton, Secret Agent**

**#35 A Very Merry Christmas**

**#36 Geronimo's Valentine**

**#37 The Race Across America**

**#38 A Fabumouse School Adventure**

**#39 Singing Sensation**

**#40 The Karate Mouse**

**#41 Mighty Mount Kilimanjaro**

**#42 The Peculiar Pumpkin Thief**

**#43 I'm Not a Supermouse!**

#44 The Giant
Diamond Robbery

#45 Save the White
Whale!

#46 The Haunted
Castle

#47 Run for the Hills,
Geronimo!

#48 The Mystery in
Venice

#49 The Way of
the Samurai

#50 This Hotel Is
Haunted!

#51 The Enormouse
Pearl Heist

#52 Mouse in Space!

#53 Rumble in
the Jungle

#54 Get into Gear,
Stilton!

#55 The Golden
Statue Plot

#56 Flight of the
Red Bandit

The Hunt for the
Golden Book

#57 The Stinky
Cheese Vacation

#58 The Super
Chef Contest

#59 Welcome to
Moldy Manor

The Hunt for the
Curious Cheese

#60 The Treasure of
Easter Island

#61 Mouse House
Hunter

#62 Mouse
Overboard!

#63 The Cheese
Experiment

Join me and my friends as we travel through time in these very special editions!

## THE JOURNEY THROUGH TIME

## BACK IN TIME:
THE SECOND JOURNEY THROUGH TIME

## THE RACE AGAINST TIME:
THE THIRD JOURNEY THROUGH TIME

# Don't miss any of these exciting Thea Sisters adventures!

**Thea Stilton and the Dragon's Code**

**Thea Stilton and the Mountain of Fire**

**Thea Stilton and the Ghost of the Shipwreck**

**Thea Stilton and the Secret City**

**Thea Stilton and the Mystery in Paris**

**Thea Stilton and the Cherry Blossom Adventure**

**Thea Stilton and the Star Castaways**

**Thea Stilton: Big Trouble in the Big Apple**

**Thea Stilton and the Ice Treasure**

**Thea Stilton and the Secret of the Old Castle**

**Thea Stilton and the Blue Scarab Hunt**

**Thea Stilton and the Prince's Emerald**

**Thea Stilton and the Mystery on the Orient Express**

**Thea Stilton and the Dancing Shadows**

**Thea Stilton and the Legend of the Fire Flowers**

**Thea Stilton and the Spanish Dance Mission**

**Thea Stilton and the Journey to the Lion's Den**

**Thea Stilton and the Great Tulip Heist**

**Thea Stilton and the Chocolate Sabotage**

**Thea Stilton and the Missing Myth**

**Thea Stilton and the Lost Letters**

**Thea Stilton and the Tropical Treasure**

# MEET
# GERONIMO STILTONIX

He is a spacemouse — the Geronimo Stilton of a parallel universe! He is captain of the spaceship *MouseStar 1*. While flying through the cosmos, he visits distant planets and meets crazy aliens. His adventures are out of this world!

#1 Alien Escape

#2 You're Mine, Captain!

#3 Ice Planet Adventure

#4 The Galactic Goal

#5 Rescue Rebellion

#6 The Underwater Planet

# Be sure to read all of our magical special edition adventures!

**THE KINGDOM OF FANTASY**

**THE QUEST FOR PARADISE:**
THE RETURN TO THE KINGDOM OF FANTASY

**THE AMAZING VOYAGE:**
THE THIRD ADVENTURE IN THE KINGDOM OF FANTASY

**THE DRAGON PROPHECY:**
THE FOURTH ADVENTURE IN THE KINGDOM OF FANTASY

**THE VOLCANO OF FIRE:**
THE FIFTH ADVENTURE IN THE KINGDOM OF FANTASY

**THE SEARCH FOR TREASURE:**
THE SIXTH ADVENTURE IN THE KINGDOM OF FANTASY

**THE ENCHANTED CHARMS**
THE SEVENTH ADVENTURE IN THE KINGDOM OF FANTASY

**THE PHOENIX OF DESTINY:**
AN EPIC KINGDOM OF FANTASY ADVENTURE

**THEA STILTON: THE JOURNEY TO ATLANTIS**

**THEA STILTON: THE SECRET OF THE FAIRIES**

**THEA STILTON: THE SECRET OF THE SNOW**

**THEA STILTON: THE CLOUD CASTLE**

1. Mountains of the Mangy Yeti
2. Cacklefur Castle
3. Angry Walnut Tree
4. Rattenbaum Mansion
5. Rancidrat River
6. Bridge of Shaky Steps
7. Squeakspeare Mansion
8. Slimy Swamp
9. Ogre Highway
10. Gloomeria
11. Shivery Arts Academy
12. Horrorwood Studios

# CACKLEFUR CASTLE

1. Oozing moat

2. Drawbridge

3. Grand entrance

4. Moldy basement

5. Patio, with a view of the moat

6. Dusty library

7. Room for unwanted guests

8. Mummy room

9. Watchtower

10. Creaking staircase

11. Banquet room

12. Garage (for antique hearses)

13. Bewitched tower

14. Garden of carnivorous plants

15. Stinky kitchen

16. Crocodile pool and piranha tank

17. Creepella's room

18. Tower of musky tarantulas

19. Bitewing's tower (with antique contraptions)

# DEAR MOUSE FRIENDS, GOOD-BYE UNTIL THE NEXT BOOK!